My Grandson is a Genius!

by Giles Andreae

illustrated by Sue Hellard

BLOOMSBURY
CHILDREN'S
BOOKS

travel cot

For Grandman – G.A.

For Philippa – S.H.

First published in Great Britain in 2003 by Bloomsbury Publishing Plc
38 Soho Square, London, W1D 3HB

Text copyright © Purple Enterprises Limited 2003
Illustrations copyright © Sue Hellard 2003
The moral right of the author and illustrator has been asserted

A CIP catalogue record of this book is available from the British Library
ISBN 0 7475 5863 9

Designed by Sarah Hodder

Printed in Belgium by Proost

1 3 5 7 9 10 8 6 4 2

My grandson is a genius!
It's plain for all to see,
I'm sure it won't be long
Before he sits for a degree.

I know he's only two years old
But when you watch him play,
It's obvious he'll be
A famous scientist one day.

And although it sounds unlikely,
If you heard my grandson speak,
You'd probably elect him
As Prime Minister next week.

He's clearly very musical,

'Cause when he's in his cot,
He wriggles to the rhythm
Of Puccini's Turandot.

And when you see him walking

It's embarrassingly clear

That he'll be in the Olympics
Not much later than next year.

He moves so very gracefully
For such a tender age,

And his voice is so angelic
That he'll really suit the stage.

His paintings are so masterful
You couldn't fail to tell
That my grandson and Picasso
Would have got on very well.

And when he kicks a football

You'd be hard put to deny

That any player ever

Has had such a brilliant eye.

Though I'm not much one for boasting,

If you saw his little face,
You'd agree that they should use him
To promote the human race.

Yes, my grandson is a genius
And, though I'm not sure I'd agree,
His parents sometimes say
That he's a little bit like me!